The Hamster Who Got Himself Stuck

Other books in this series:
The Cat Who Smelled Like Cabbage
The Dog Who Loved to Race
The Parrot Who Talked Too Much

Cover design by Durand Demlow
Illustrations by Anne Gavitt

Published by Multnomah Press
10209 SE Division Street
Portland, Oregon 97266

Multnomah Press is a ministry of Multnomah School of the Bible, 8435 NE Glisan Street, Portland, Oregon 97220.

Printed in Singapore.

Library of Congress Cataloging-in-Publication Data

Jackson, Neta.
The hamster who got himself stuck / Neta Jackson.
p. cm. —(Pet parables)
Summary: Marble, the biggest, oldest, and bossiest hamster in the litter, comes to realize that sharing things with his brothers and sisters can be fun. Includes a Bible verse and discussion questions.
ISBN 0-88070-416-0
[1. Hamsters—Fiction. 2. Brothers and sisters—Fiction. 3. Sharing—Fiction. 4. Parables.] I. Title. II Series: Jackson, Neta. Pet parables.
PZ7.J13684Ham 1990
[E]—dc20 90-48384
CIP
AC

91 92 93 94 95 96 97 98 99 - 10 9 8 7 6 5 4 3 2 1

The Hamster Who Got Himself Stuck

Neta Jackson

Illustrated by Anne Gavitt

MULTNOMAH

Portland, Oregon 97266

Marble burrowed under the cedar shavings of the hamster cage and hid quietly until one of his hamster brothers came sniffing past.

"Gotcha!" yelled Marble as he burst from his hideout and bowled over the other baby hamster.

"Marble!" wailed Wee Willie. "Just 'cause you're bigger than me, you always knock me over!"

Marble grinned to himself and scurried away. It was so much fun knocking over his runty little brother.

Hearing the running wheel go squeak, squeak, Marble scampered along the plastic tube that connected the two parts of the big, rambling hamster cage. On the other side, his brothers and sisters were taking turns running around in the big wheel. Sometimes two or three would try to run at once. The baby hamsters squealed, fell over each other, and laughingly got back in the wheel.

Marble pushed his way onto the wheel. "It's my turn!" he bullied. He pushed off a sister, then started to run.

"Marble!" the other hamsters protested. "You butted in!" But Marble just ran and ran. The wheel went faster and faster.

"I can run fast because I'm big like my daddy," Marble thought. Daddy hamster was a large gold and white Teddy Bear Hamster. Out of a litter of eight baby hamsters, Marble was the only one who was gold and white. All the rest of his brothers and sisters were tan like their mother, who was a Golden Hamster.

After awhile Marble got tired and stopped. He looked around, but no one was there. All his brothers and sisters had given up and gone away. Marble shrugged. Oh, well. He hopped off the wheel and scampered back through the plastic tube. Some of the litter were crowded around Mother hamster getting dinner. Marble headed for the water bottle. Wee Willie was nosing the end of the tube which let water dribble out a little at a time.

"Get out of the way," Marble demanded. "I'm hot and I need a drink."

"But I was here first," the smaller hamster protested.

"But I'm the oldest so I should get to drink before you," Marble said. And he pushed Wee Willie away and drank a long time.

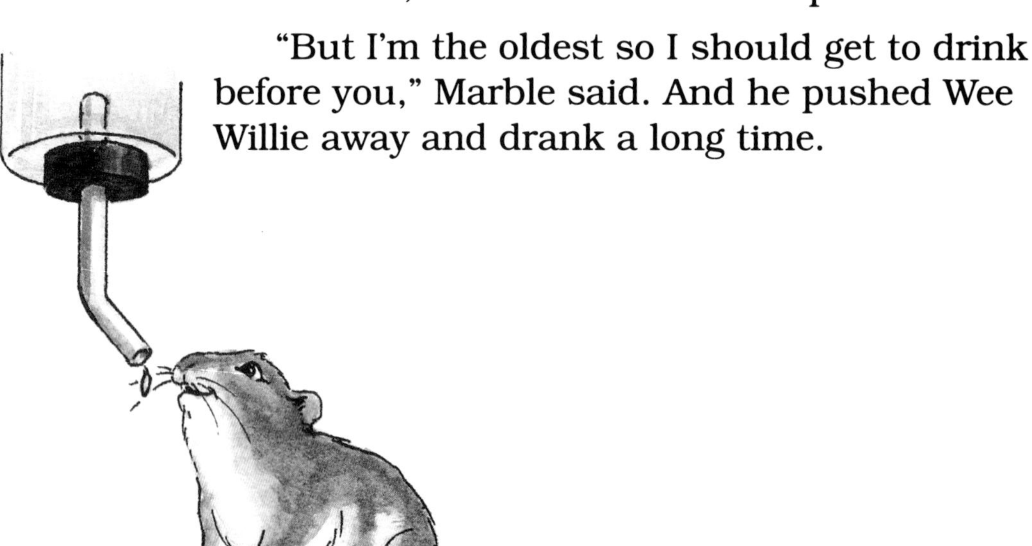

Just then Daddy hamster came down the long, tall tube that led straight up to the feeding platform where the People put food for the grown-up hamsters. The big gold and white Teddy Bear Hamster touched noses with his look-alike offspring, then curled up in a nest of torn tissue for a nap.

Marble went over and stretched up to the opening of the tube. He was sure he was big enough to climb up to the feeding platform. After all, he was a Teddy Bear Hamster just like his daddy, and he was the biggest and the best! But he wanted to practice when no one was looking, so Marble decided to just curl up in the nest of torn tissue and take a nap, too.

The next morning Marble heard some noises. He peeked out of the nest and saw that the cover of the hamster cage was off. The People were putting new food into the feeding platform—lots and lots of food!

"There," he heard the People say, "that should be enough food for Goldie and Teddy while we're gone for the weekend." Then the cover was put back on, a door slammed, and everything was quiet.

Marble crept out of the nest. Everyone else was still sleeping. He felt a thrill of excitement. He was going to go up the tube to the feeding platform! Up he stretched to the opening of the tube and got a grip with his paws. Up, up he climbed. Once he slipped a little, but caught himself on the ridges, took a breath, and kept climbing. Finally he poked his nose over the top and stared in surprise.

What a feast! Slices of apples, crunchy lettuce, lots of sunflower seeds and pellets, even a long orange carrot. Marble didn't know where to start! He tried the carrot. Oh! It was so crisp and crunchy. He ate and ate. Then he nibbled on the lettuce. It was so sweet! He tasted the apple. Marble thought he had never tasted anything so good. Before he knew it, the apple slice was all gone.

Now what? Marble chewed on some of the crunchy pellets. Not so exciting, but it made him feel grownup and important.

Marble kept eating and eating. Suddenly he began to feel a little strange.

Maybe I should stop now, he thought. The longer he sat, the sicker he felt.

He didn't want to be up on the feeding platform any more. He wanted his mother. Marble crawled to the opening of the tube. But as he looked down, he felt very dizzy. He shook all over. He felt so stuffed that he could hardly move. He was miserable.

Marble didn't know how long he lay there. But after awhile he was aware of his mother's nose poking out of the top of the tube.

"Marble! What are you doing up here?" she asked.

Marble just groaned.

"You have to move over. I can't come up," she said.

"I can't," Marble moaned.

Mother hamster looked around at all the nibbled food. She looked at Marble. Now she knew what the trouble was. She didn't say anything, but just backed down the tube.

Marble wanted to call for her to come back. But he felt too sick to even squeak. He just lay there.

Pretty soon he heard the squeak, squeak, squeak of the wheel going around and around. Marble wished he was down in the cage playing with his brothers and sisters. But the thought of going around and around in the wheel made him feel dizzy. So Marble tried to not think about it.

All day long he could hear sounds from below. No one came to see him. His mother and daddy couldn't come up to the feeding platform because he was in the way. His brothers and sisters couldn't climb up. Marble felt very lonely.

Nighttime came and Marble slept. All the next day he slept and woke, slept and woke. He got very thirsty, but there was no water on the feeding platform. After a long time he realized the cover of the hamster cage was being lifted. A People hand picked him up and set him down gently in the bottom of the cage. Mother hamster came over and nosed him all over. Then she picked him up by the scruff of the neck and dragged him over to the nest. Marble felt so glad to be back in the cage that he forgot to feel embarrassed that his mother was treating him like a baby.

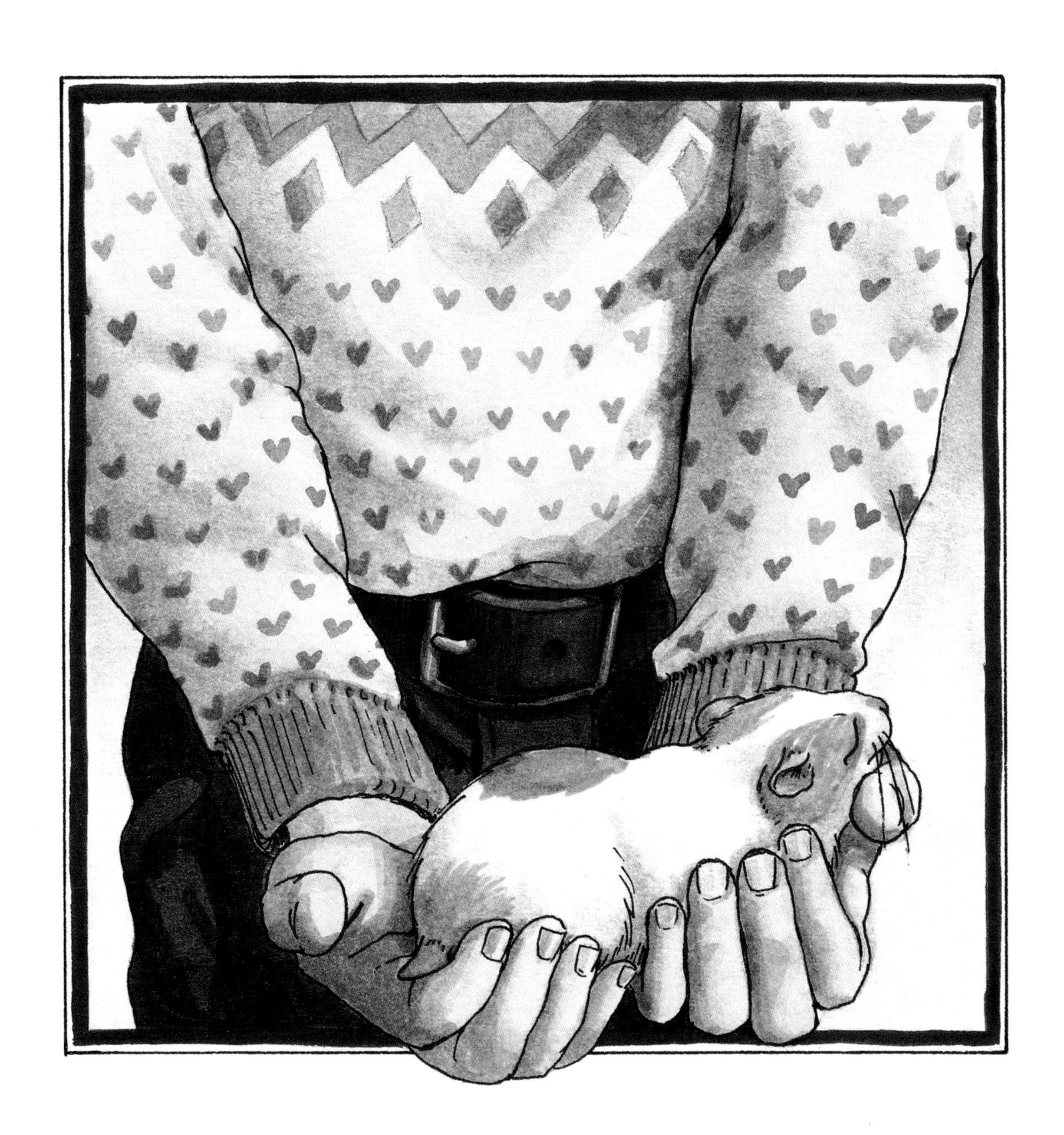

Marble still didn't feel too good, so he stayed in the nest all the next day. His brothers and sisters came over from time to time to look at him curiously.

"I'm sorry you're sick, Marble," one said.

"I hope you feel better soon," said another. Then they scampered off to play.

"I'm thirsty," Marble whispered.

No one heard him except Wee Willie. Without a word, the smaller hamster went over to the water bottle and took a drink. Then he came back to the nest and dribbled some water on Marble's paws. Marble licked the water gratefully. In a moment, his little brother was back again with a few more drops. Back and forth went the little hamster between the water bottle and the nest until Marble wasn't thirsty anymore.

Marble felt ashamed. He was always pushing Wee Willie around. Somehow it didn't seem like fun any more. "I'm sorry I pushed you away from the water bottle," he said to Wee Willie.

Wee Willie didn't know what to say, so he just touched noses with Marble and scurried away. Marble sighed and closed his eyes. Being the oldest and the biggest didn't necessarily mean being the best, he decided. Wee Willie was the smallest hamster in the litter, but he was pretty nice. As Marble thought about how his little brother shared his water, he fell fast asleep.

The next morning Marble felt as good as new! As soon as his mother checked him all over to make sure he was okay, Marble scooted through the plastic tube into the next cage.

Squeak, squeak, squeak went the running wheel. Marble was so eager to play that he almost rushed right up to the wheel. But then he remembered. Being the oldest and biggest didn't mean he should push his brothers and sisters around. So Marble waited for his turn. When he got on the wheel, he ran faster and faster.

“Look at Marble go!” all the hamsters cheered. Marble felt good. After awhile he stopped and let Wee Willie get on the wheel with him. Faster and faster went the wheel. It went so fast that Wee Willie fell off. Marble stopped anxiously. Was his little brother hurt? But Wee Willie was laughing.

Marble laughed, too. It was more fun to play together than to push his brothers and sisters around. As he got off the wheel so someone else could have a turn, Marble thought, “It’s fun to share!”

“Whoever wants to become great among you must be your servant” (Matthew 20:26).

To the Parent

"Me first! Me first!"

Sound familiar? Children are naturally focused on their own needs and desires, whether it's who gets the biggest piece of cake or who gets to play with the truck. They also learn quickly that if you're bigger or older, you have an advantage in getting your own way—or conversely, if you're littler or younger, you have to fight to get your share.

But just looking out for Number One can be lonely and not very much fun. Kids who grab what they want, refuse to share, and push others out of the way are soon avoided. It's important to help our children realize that sharing means everyone gets to have fun, that you don't have to be "biggest" or "best" to be a great person.

After reading the story of Marble and the hamster family aloud to your child, you may want to use the following questions to discuss what happens in our relationships when we think we deserve more than other people deserve.

1. Why did Marble think he was the best baby hamster in the whole litter?
2. Why did he always push Wee Willie around?
3. Who had fun when Marble pushed Wee Willie around? Who didn't have fun?
4. What did the other baby hamsters do when Marble jumped on the running wheel even though it wasn't his turn?
5. Why did Marble get stuck up on the feeding platform?
6. How did he feel while he was stuck?
7. How did Marble feel when Wee Willie brought him some water when he was sick?
8. Why did Marble decide not to push Wee Willie around any more?
9. What happened when Marble waited for his turn to play on the running wheel? Who had fun this time?